Digby and Kate Again

by Barbara Baker

pictures by
Marsha Winborn

E. P. DUTTON   NEW YORK

for Jeanne, Charlie,

and Chris

B.A.B.

Text copyright © 1989 by Barbara A. Baker
Illustrations copyright © 1989 by Marsha Winborn

Library of Congress Cataloging-in-Publication Data
Baker, Barbara, date
   Digby and Kate again.
   Summary: Digby the dog and Kate the cat share four
adventures: hunting, bicycling, letter writing,
and raking leaves.
   [1. Friendship—Fiction.   2. Dogs—Fiction.
3. Cats—Fiction]   I. Winborn, Marsha, ill.   II. Title.
PZ7.B16922Dk   1989   [E]   88-25677
ISBN 0-525-44477-7

Published in the United States by
E. P. Dutton, a division of
Penguin Books USA Inc.

Published simultaneously in Canada by
Fitzhenry & Whiteside Limited, Toronto

Printed in Hong Kong

First Edition   10 9 8 7 6 5 4 3 2

CONTENTS

DIGBY'S GARDEN

One day Digby was working in his garden.

All morning he dug in the soil,

and pulled weeds, and watered plants.

"Now I will stop," said Digby.

"I will rest in the shade."

"Hello, Digby," said Kate.

She looked at Digby's garden.

Bees hummed.

Flies buzzed.

Ants crawled.

"This is a great garden," said Kate.

"Thank you," said Digby.

"Great for hunting!" said Kate.

A dragonfly flew past.

Kate jumped.

"Rats," she said.

"I missed it."

"Come on, Digby," said Kate.

"Let's go hunting."

"Not me," said Digby.

"I do not want to hunt.

I want to rest in the shade."

Kate chased a fly—

round and round,

in and out.

"I almost got it," she said.

"Please come and hunt with me, Digby.

Hunting is fun."

She tried to pull him up.

"Oh, all right," said Digby.

11

He got up.

He went into the garden.

Kate ran off.

She tried to catch a beetle.

But it got away.

She tried to catch an ant.

It got away too.

"I cannot catch anything today,"

said Kate.

"Maybe this garden

is *not* so great for hunting."

"Kate," called Digby.

"I got something.

Come and see."

"What did you get?" asked Kate.

"Look," said Digby.

"I got a bone."

Digby took his bone to a shady spot.

He started to chew it.

"You are right, Kate," he said.

"My garden *is* great for hunting."

THE BICYCLE

Kate had a new red bicycle.

"Wow!" said Digby.

"Would you like to try it?" asked Kate.

Digby looked at the bicycle.

"I do not know how to ride a bike,"

he said sadly.

"It is easy," said Kate.

"I will help you."

"You are a good friend," said Digby.

He got on the bike.

"You hold the seat

while I ride," said Digby.

"Okay," said Kate.

Digby pushed the pedals.

The bike began to move.

Kate held on. She ran.

The bike went faster.

Kate let go.

The bike began to wiggle.

"Digby," cried Kate,

"you have to make it go straight."

"I do not know *how,*" cried Digby.

CRASH!

Kate pulled Digby up.

"Try again, Digby," she said.

"It's easy."

Digby tried again.

It was *not* easy.

He tried again,

and again,

and again.

He fell many times.

Finally Digby said,

"I think I can do it by myself now, Kate."

He started to pedal.

The bike went fast—

and faster.

"Hooray!" cried Digby.

"Look at me."

"You did it!" said Kate.

"You rode my bike."

"Yes," said Digby. "I did.

Now it is your turn, Kate."

Digby sat down to rest.

Kate got on her bike.

"Go ahead," said Digby.

"I will watch you."

"Digby," said Kate. "I cannot go ahead.

I do not know how

to ride a bike."

KATE'S LETTER

"I do not like to write letters,"

said Kate.

"But today I must write a thank-you letter

to Aunt Hazel."

Kate got paper and a pencil.

She sat down.

"Dear Aunt Hazel," she wrote.

Kate stopped.

"I am hungry," she said.

"First I will eat breakfast.

Then I will write to Aunt Hazel."

Kate had cornflakes and milk.

"That was good," she said.

"Now I can start my letter—

as soon as I wash the dishes."

Kate washed the dishes.

She put them on the shelf.

"This shelf is messy," she said.

"I will fix it up.

Then I can write my letter."

Kate took everything

off the shelf.

"I will clean out the cabinets too,"

she said.

Kate took everything

out of the cabinets.

She found a can of paint.

"Oh, good," said Kate.

"I can paint my shelf.

That will look nice.

But where is my paintbrush?

Maybe it is in my closet."

Kate looked in her bedroom closet.

She found lots of things.

But she did not find her paintbrush.

"Maybe I put it in my dresser."

Kate opened the dresser drawers.

"What a mess," she said.

She pulled the clothes out

and put them on her bed.

"I will fold these clothes

and put them back," Kate said.

"But first I will look for my paintbrush

under the bed."

Kate found her slippers

under the bed.

She found one boot,

and a flashlight,

and two yellow pencils,

and three missing checkers,

and one spiderweb,

and lots of dust.

She crawled out.

Someone was ringing her doorbell.

It was Digby.

"Hello, Digby," said Kate.

Digby looked around.

"Wow!" he said.

"What are you doing in here, Kate?"

"Oh," said Kate,

"I am just writing a letter

to my Aunt Hazel."

FALL LEAVES

"What can we do today?" said Kate.

"*I* have to rake leaves," said Digby.

"Oh," said Kate.

She looked around.

Leaves were everywhere.

Millions of leaves.

Red leaves, orange leaves,

brown leaves, yellow leaves.

"I do not think

raking all these leaves

will be fun," said Kate.

"No," said Digby.

"It will not be fun."

He got a rake.

He started working.

"I have an idea," said Kate.

"I will help you rake the leaves.

Then we will have time

to do something fun."

"That is a good idea," said Digby.

Kate and Digby worked and worked.

They raked all the leaves

into a great big pile.

"Look," said Kate,

"we made a big hill."

"Yes," said Digby.

"We worked very hard.

Now it is time to have fun.

But what can we do?"

Kate did not say anything.

She was looking at the hill of leaves.

Her tail twitched.

"Oh, no," said Digby.

Kate started to walk

toward the hill.

"Stop, Kate!" cried Digby.

"Don't do it."

But Digby was too late.

Kate jumped.

Leaves flew everywhere.

Millions of leaves.

Red leaves, orange leaves,

brown leaves, yellow leaves.

"Ohhh," groaned Digby.

"Come on in," said Kate.

"This is lots of fun."

Digby looked at the hill of leaves.

Millions of leaves.

Red leaves, orange leaves,

brown leaves, yellow leaves.

And he jumped in too.